First published in the UK in 2000 by

Belitha Press Ltd
London House, Great Eastern Wharf,
Parkgate Road, London SW11 4NQ

ISBN 1 84138 125 X

British Library Cataloguing in Publication Data
for this book is available from the British Library.

Editor: Stephanie Turnbull
Designer: Zoë Quayle
Educational consultant: Margaret Bellwood

Printed in Singapore

CONTENTS

ANCIENT EGYPT

**Most of Egypt is hot, dry desert where nothing grows.
However, the River Nile flows through the country, from top
to bottom, and the lands around the Nile are lush and green.
This is where the first Egyptians settled over 5,000 years ago.**

For over 3,000 years Egypt was one of the richest and most powerful
civilizations in the world. Today, it is famous for its ancient pyramids.
These were the treasure-filled tombs of the pharaohs (kings), whom
the Ancient Egyptians thought were living gods. The Ancient Egyptians
also built huge temples and statues to honour the pharaohs, and they
wrote stories about the gods and goddesses they worshipped.

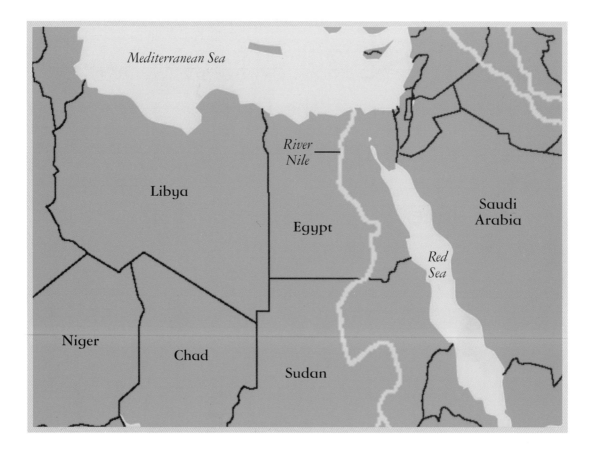

Over the centuries, as people from different parts of Egypt travelled across the country, they spread their own stories and beliefs. Their ideas often mixed together. For instance, Egyptians began to worship the sun god, Ra, and the creator god, Atum, as one: Ra-Atum. The stories we know today are a combination of these tales from different parts of Ancient Egypt.

The walls and treasures of the Ancient Egyptians' fabulous temples and tombs were decorated with hieroglyphs, a special kind of writing made up of tiny letter and picture symbols. It is these hieroglyphs that tell the original stories behind the magical tales in this book.

This is a symbol called the wadjet eye. It represents the eye of the god Horus. Ancient Egyptians believed that it had special powers to keep away evil.

THE END OF HUMANKIND

Before time began, the great god Ra lived all by himself
in an ocean of dark emptiness. There was no one to
talk to and nothing to see. Ra was lonely and bored.
He began to think… and his thoughts were so powerful
that they brought things to life.

First, Ra made other gods and goddesses to keep him
company. He set the earth god down below and the sky
god up above. Then Ra made mountains and rivers,
animals and birds, reptiles and fish, trees and plants.
He wept tears that turned into humans. He lit up the
sky with his own light, the golden glow of the sun.
Ra had created the world. He loved it so much that he
went to live there in his favourite country, Egypt.

At first, men and women lived in fear of the mighty
ruler of the world. They built Ra huge temples and
prayed and sang hymns and offered sacrifices.

As the years passed, Ra grew old. His skin glimmered
like thin gold. His bones gleamed like pale silver and
his hair glittered blue-grey. Finally, Ra no longer looked
like the great creator of everyone and everything. The
all-powerful lord of the gods was just like a frail, old man.

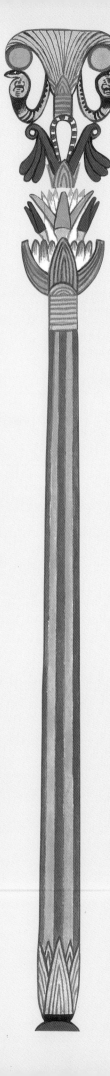

When the people noticed this, they started to lose their respect for Ra.

'This old god will soon be gone,' people began to murmur. 'Why should we follow him any more? Why should we still do what he says? Let's find a way to be rid of him, then we can rule ourselves.'

Ra was furious when he found out what his humans were plotting. He ordered all the gods and goddesses to come at once to a secret meeting in his palace.

'The humans who came from my tears are turning against me!' Ra thundered. 'Shall I forgive these ungrateful creatures or punish them?'

'Wipe away these tears!' bellowed one of the gods. 'Kill them all!'

'Yes!' roared Ra. 'You are right! I shall destroy the whole human race!'

The gods and goddesses bowed in agreement.

The raging Ra then turned to his daughter, the moon goddess Hathor.

'Hathor, I want you to turn yourself into a lioness!' he commanded. 'Go and gobble up these people!'

'I will, Father,' said Hathor obediently.

The gods and goddesses watched as Hathor crouched down on all fours. Her skin began to turn golden and furry.

Her body arched into that of a huge, wild cat. Her hands and feet spread into enormous paws with long, cruel claws. Whiskers twitched at Hathor's pointed nose. She sniffed the air hungrily. Then she opened her razor-toothed jaws and snarled. With one mighty leap, she sprang off in search of her supper...

As Hathor roamed over the earth, the people ran to and fro in a panic. Hour after hour, Hathor hunted them down. She pounced and grabbed and slashed and tore and munched and crunched. By the time the sun set, thousands of men, women and children lay dead. Hathor padded back to Ra's palace with her stomach full and her fur matted with blood.

I'll finish the job tomorrow, she thought to herself and settled down to sleep, licking her lips dreamily.

Ra himself didn't feel so pleased. All day long he had listened to his humans screaming and crying in terror – and not just guilty people, but innocent ones too. Ra felt terrible. Now his anger had cooled, he realized he had gone too far. But it was too late. He had given Hathor her orders and he couldn't go back on his word, or everyone would think that he was weaker than ever.

As Ra sat glumly on his throne with his head in his hands, he suddenly thought of a way to put things right.

9

There wasn't a moment to lose! While the exhausted Hathor snored, Ra commanded his servants to bring him hundreds of sacks of red earth. Next, he told his high priest and the slave girls of the temple to mix the earth with seven thousand jars of barley beer. Then Ra silently led the high priest and slave girls out into the night. They carried the jars to the spot where Hathor had finished killing. Ra ordered everyone to pour the dark, red liquid on to the ground. As soon as the last jar was empty, everyone slipped away unseen.

Next morning, Hathor woke up ready to have a fine feast of humans for her breakfast. With a loud roar, she sprang out of Ra's palace once again and leapt across the earth.

She hadn't gone far before – splash! Her paws landed in a large, dark, red pool that looked like blood. Hathor was delighted! She began to lap up the liquid as eagerly as a cat laps up milk.

Mmmmm! Hathor thought. *It tastes even better than the blood I drank yesterday!*

Hathor drank and drank and drank. The red liquid tasted so delicious that she didn't notice her head becoming fuzzy, her eyes getting blurry and her arms and legs getting heavy and tired. Hathor was drunk!

Her thoughts became muddled and she forgot all about Ra's orders to kill everyone. Instead she staggered back to the palace with a sleepy smile on her face.

'Hello – hic – father,' she hiccupped and sank down at the foot of Ra's throne. Hathor rested her head on Ra's lap and he gently stroked her head. Then Hathor closed her sleepy eyelids and fell into a deep, contented sleep.

Ra was content too. He hadn't gone back on his order to Hathor, but the human race had been saved.

To this very day, when the River Nile floods, the waters rush over the red earth of Egypt and the river runs the colour of blood. It is Ra's reminder to humans not to turn against him again.

THE SECRET NAME OF RA

After humans had turned against Ra, the mighty sun god didn't want to live among people any more, so he made his home in the sky instead.

Every day, Ra sailed across the sky in a huge boat of blazing light and watched the world below. Each evening, the sun boat sank down under the earth to the Kingdom of the West, where the souls of the dead lived. Ra used strong magic to protect himself and his boat from the dangers of the underworld. Every morning, the mighty ruler of the world came sailing safely back up into the sky.

Ra had built a great palace for himself in his favourite country, Egypt. Now he no longer needed this earthly home, but he was sad to see the splendid building standing silent, still and empty. So he gave his palace to a god called Osiris and a goddess called Isis. Ra made them king and queen of Egypt. He ordered them to look after his people and take care of the whole world.

Isis was perhaps the most clever of all the gods and goddesses. She knew all about every living thing in heaven and earth. She knew the secret of making things grow. She knew a million different magic spells.

In fact there was just one thing that Isis didn't know –
Ra's secret name. Ra could take on many different
forms and so humans gave him all kinds of names.
They were great titles such as The Rising Sun, The Setting
Sun, The Moulder of Mountains and The All. But none
of these was Ra's *real* name. Ra's real name was the best
kept secret in the universe. Only he knew what it was.
Ra's secret name was the key to all his power.

Isis knew that if she could find out Ra's secret name,
she would have control over the mighty lord of the gods.
But even though Isis knew some of the strongest magic
in the world, she couldn't use her spells to find out this
name. Her magic wouldn't work against Ra, the creator
of everyone and everything. So Isis decided she would
have to discover the secret name by trickery instead.

One day, when Ra was strolling across the Earth, Isis
saw her chance. The elderly sun god had started to hobble
as he walked and he sometimes dribbled out of the side
of his mouth. As Ra stopped to talk to some other gods
and goddesses, a little spot of dribble dripped on to the
earth. Quick as a flash, Isis scooped up the damp soil
without anyone noticing. She smiled gleefully to herself.
One drop of the creator's own spit would be more
powerful against him than any magic spells.

Isis hurried back to her palace and locked herself away in her chamber. She kneaded and pounded and pinched the damp soil until it looked just like a snake. Isis put her model down on the floor and stood back, murmuring words of magic. Suddenly the snake wriggled into life. It hissed and flickered its forked tongue.

Isis carried the snake to one of Ra's favourite spots. Then she whispered instructions to it and let it loose on the sand. The snake quickly slithered away and Isis calmly returned to her palace.

Next day, Ra was enjoying an early morning walk when he felt a sharp jab in his ankle. He was so shocked that he didn't notice something sliding away into the shadows. The snake had crept up and bitten Ra! A terrible burning sensation began to flood through the sun god's foot and up his leg. He fell to the ground, screaming in pain.

'Help!' Ra howled. 'Something has poisoned me! I do not know what it was, for nothing I have created is able to hurt me... Hurry! I am growing weak!'

All the other gods and goddesses came running in a panic. They crowded round with anxious faces.

'How can this be happening?' they gasped.

Of course, Isis knew just what had happened, but she pretended to be just as horrified as everyone else.

Ra was pale and sweating. He shook uncontrollably as the poison spread through his body.

'Help me! I am dying,' he groaned fearfully.

One by one, the gods and goddesses tried to use their magic to cure Ra. But one by one, they all failed. They wailed and wrung their hands in despair.

'My lord, I know a spell that will heal you,' said Isis craftily. 'However, it won't work unless I have the power of your secret name.'

'My name is The All,' Ra whispered weakly through dry lips. 'I am The Rising Sun and The Setting Sun. I am The Moulder of Mountains...'

'No, no, my lord,' Isis insisted. 'If you want me to save you, you must tell me your secret name.'

Ra closed his eyes in torment. The pain was becoming too bad to bear.

'Come close, Isis,' Ra croaked. 'I will tell you my secret name, but you must promise never to reveal it to anyone!'

Isis could hardly contain her excitement.

'I promise,' she breathed, her eyes glittering with delight.

And Ra whispered to Isis his secret name.

At last Isis had the power she wanted! She was so overjoyed that she not only cured Ra of the snakebite, but she also made the aged sun god young again.

Suddenly Ra was as bright and shining as he had been at the start of time. Everyone wept tears of gladness as he climbed into his sun boat and sailed into the sky. The great creator was well again!

Today in Egypt there are many ancient temples and monuments built to the glory of Ra. They are covered in writing which praises the mighty sun god and lists his many names. There are hundreds of stories about Ra carved into columns and painted on tomb walls. There are thousands of records written on paper scrolls. But none of these – not one – tells the secret name of Ra. Isis kept her promise well.

THE MURDER OF A GOD

The god Osiris and the goddess Isis ruled Egypt wisely. They loved their country and did everything they could to make the lives of their people better. Osiris and Isis showed the Egyptians the best way to farm the land. They brought law and order to the country. They also taught the people how to worship the other gods properly, so the gods were pleased and treated the people kindly in return.

Egypt grew to be a rich, happy place and the time came when Osiris decided that he should help other countries too. So the king said goodbye to his beautiful queen and beloved homeland and set off on a long journey around the world.

Everyone in Egypt was sad to see Osiris go – except for Osiris' brother, the god Seth. Seth was desperately jealous because the mighty sun god Ra had chosen Osiris to be the king of Egypt, rather than him, Seth. He was determined somehow to take the throne from his brother. Seth knew he couldn't just fight Osiris, because the Egyptians loved and supported their king and wouldn't accept Seth as ruler instead.

Seth knew that he'd have to get rid of Osiris in secret...

Now Osiris was away, Seth saw his chance to make a move. Isis was ruling the country single-handedly. She was far too busy to keep an eye on him. Sneakily, Seth started to gather supporters.

'If you help me to be king of Egypt, I will reward you richly,' he whispered to certain courtiers. The greedy courtiers smiled. They liked the sound of that! They promised to help Seth whenever he gave the word.

Eventually Osiris returned home to Egypt. The people were so happy they sang and danced in the streets. Seth was asked to a special celebration at the palace. The wicked god rubbed his hands in glee. Isis wasn't going to be at the feast, so it was the perfect time for him to put his plan into action...

The palace was beautifully decorated for the banquet with garlands and banners and perfumed candles. Hundreds of guests enjoyed mouth-watering food and delicious wine. After dinner, there were dancers and acrobats and jugglers... and then Seth clapped his hands for silence.

'Brother,' he announced to Osiris, 'in honour of your return, I have organized a little entertainment of my own for you. I hope you enjoy it.'

Seth clapped his hands again and the huge palace doors swung wide open. A group of courtiers staggered in, carrying a long, narrow, golden chest on their shoulders. They set the heavy, beautiful box down in the middle of the room. It gleamed like the sun and was decorated with carvings and jewels.

As Osiris and his guests stood open-mouthed, marvelling at the stunning treasure, Seth smirked to himself. The chest was part of his evil plot. He had already told the courtiers exactly what to do and just when to do it...

'Here's the game,' Seth laughed. 'Let's see if anyone can fit inside this chest exactly – head touching one end, feet the other. Whoever fits in best can keep the chest as his prize!'

A murmur of delight went round the room and everyone dashed across to the chest to have a go. The courtiers organized everyone into an orderly queue and helped each person to take their turn.

It was no good. Some were too tall for the chest, others were too short or too fat. In the end, everyone except King Osiris himself had tried unsuccessfully to fit into the golden box.

'Brother,' said Seth, 'will you not join the fun?'

Osiris paused for a moment. Then he smiled.

'Why not!' he said.

As the king stepped into the chest, the courtiers stood round it so none of the guests could see. Osiris lay down. To his surprise, he fitted perfectly! Yet it was no surprise to Seth, who had made the chest exactly the right size to fit the king. And it wasn't really a chest. It was a coffin...

Seth, the coffin and Osiris were hidden from view by the courtiers. While the guests chatted and joked around them, Seth slammed down the coffin lid and bolted it in place. Then the courtiers fell back, leaving the closed box quiet and still. It looked to everyone as if the king must have climbed out of the chest and walked away.

'No one fitted the chest!' lied Seth. 'The prize remains my own.'

With that, the wicked courtiers heaved the chest back on to their shoulders and carried it from the room with Osiris trapped inside.

Osiris fitted so snugly in the coffin that there was no room for him to raise his arms or lift his legs to thump on the sides. The golden box was so thick that no one heard his cries for help. The chest was sealed so tightly that there was hardly any air. The panicking Osiris began to sweat as it became harder and harder to breathe.

With a last, muffled gasp for help, the king of Egypt died.

In the pitch black of the night, Seth's helpers secretly carried the coffin to the River Nile and heaved it into the water. Next morning, Seth announced the tragic death of his brother. While the whole of Egypt mourned, Seth gleefully proclaimed himself king and was crowned that very day.

Seth was triumphant. He was sure he had tricked everyone. But the wise Isis hadn't been fooled. She was determined to find out exactly how her husband had died and what had happened to his body...

THE SEARCH FOR OSIRIS

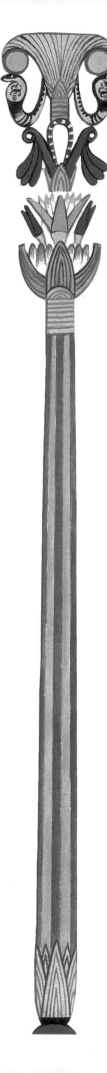

After the mysterious death of Osiris, Queen Isis disguised herself as an ordinary Egyptian and wandered all over Egypt searching for her beloved husband's body. She heard and saw nothing that could explain what had happened, until she came across a group of children playing in a village by the River Nile.

The children told Isis they had seen some men creep down to the water late one night and throw in a golden chest. They had heard them boasting that the dead king was inside. The men had gone away, thinking that the chest had sunk, but the children had seen it bob up to the surface and float away downstream.

Isis hurried hopefully along the bank of the Nile, her eyes fixed on the waters. When the broad river widened into the huge, blue ocean, Isis followed the frothing waves around the coastline. The beautiful goddess passed through country after country in her search, but there was never any sign of something golden in the water. Still Isis didn't give up. She sometimes heard local people telling of a strange and magnificent chest floating along in the sea and the tales spurred her on.

Eventually Isis reached the kingdom of Byblos. As she hurried along the beach, she heard some fishermen discussing an unusual story of a huge tree that had sprung up overnight on the shore. The king of Byblos had taken the strong, handsome tree to his palace and made it into a mighty pillar. Isis stopped in her tracks. Her heart began to beat faster.

Surely the magical tree must have something to do with Osiris? she thought. Excitedly, she made her way to the palace.

The queen's maids soon heard that a beautiful, elegant woman had arrived from a distant country. The girls took Isis to meet the queen, who loved to hear gossip from faraway places. The queen of Byblos was enchanted by Isis' elegant hairstyle, beautiful clothes and charming conversation. She begged Isis to stay in the palace and become her special companion. Isis was thrilled.

That night, Isis crept into the room where the new pillar stood. The moment she touched the smooth wood, her fingers tingled with magic and she knew what had happened to her husband. The coffin had been washed ashore and had stuck in the tangled roots of a young tree. The dead god's magic power had leaked out and the tree had suddenly sprung up tall around the coffin.

Isis realized that Osiris' body was in the centre of the wooden pillar! The goddess didn't breathe a word of the truth to anyone. She was content to be able to stay in the palace, close by her dead husband.

As time passed, the queen of Byblos grew more and more fond of her new friend. She even gave Isis the special duty of looking after her baby boy. Isis came to love the child as her own son, but she was haunted by the thought that one day he would die, as Osiris had done. One night, Isis made up her mind to use her powers to stop this happening. She started a magic fire in the room where Osiris' pillar stood and she carefully placed the sleeping boy right at the centre of the flames. He didn't wake or whimper. The blaze didn't seem to touch him and Isis knew that the magic fire was burning away the child's mortality. When the spell was finished, the prince would be able to live forever.

While the magic was working, Isis turned herself into a bird and flew round and round the pillar containing the body of Osiris. Suddenly the queen came into the room. She let out an ear-splitting scream when she saw her child seemingly burning and she snatched him out of the flames. Isis at once changed back into her human form.

'Sorceress!' cried the terrified queen, 'Stay away from us!'

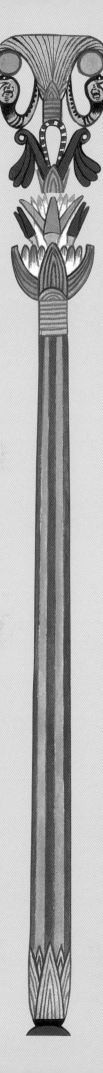

'Don't be afraid,' said Isis calmly. 'I am the goddess Isis of Egypt and I mean you no harm. If you hadn't taken your son from the magic fire, he would have been given the gift of eternal life. Now he will die one day.'

The queen hung her head in shame.

'Forgive me, Isis, for not trusting you,' she begged. 'How can I repay you for your friendship and kindness?'

Tears glistened in the goddess' eyes.

'The body of my dead husband lies inside that pillar,' she said softly. 'Please let me take him back to Egypt with me.'

Next morning, the king and queen of Byblos sadly waved farewell to Isis as she left on a boat bound for home. Also on board was the coffin, cut out from the tree. Isis stayed close by Osiris' body every minute of the long journey. As soon as the boat reached Egypt, she hid the golden coffin in the middle of a swamp where she thought no one would ever find it.

Unfortunately Seth had spies everywhere and it wasn't long before the wicked king had his hands on the chest once more. Seth knew how strong Isis' magic was and he feared that she would be able to bring Osiris back to life, so the wicked king cut up the body of Osiris into fourteen pieces. He scattered the pieces far across the land.

When Isis discovered that Osiris' body had disappeared once again, her weeping and wailing was heard all across Egypt. Even with the help of another god and goddess, it took her a long, long time to find and gather the pieces of her husband. Isis managed to make Osiris' body whole again, but all her powers failed to bring him back to life.

Isis sobbed and moaned as the mighty sun god Ra took Osiris down to the underground Kingdom of the West. There, Ra made Osiris the ruler of the dead. This honour was no consolation for the grieving Isis. Her heart was broken and cold. She was determined that Seth should pay for the terrible crime he had committed...

THE FIGHT FOR THE THRONE

The goddess Isis was in despair. She had lost everything, all because of the evil Seth. She had lost her beloved husband, Osiris. She had lost her throne and was no longer queen of Egypt. She had lost her home in the palace. She had even lost her friends, because most people were too afraid of Seth to be seen with his enemies.

Ra, the mighty creator god, took pity on the miserable goddess and decided to make her happy again. He worked a special, secret spell and gave Isis a baby boy. Isis was overjoyed. Her baby was plump and healthy – and best of all, he was the son of Osiris. The proud goddess called the boy Horus and took him to a distant part of Egypt, away from Seth's wicked clutches. Even so, Seth tried to kill the child. After all, Horus was really the rightful king of Egypt and Seth didn't want his nephew to try to claim the throne one day. However, Isis used all her magic powers to protect her only son and Horus grew up safely into a bold, brave, strong warrior.

Of course, Seth's worst fears eventually came true. When Horus was old enough, Isis told him the terrible story of his father's murder. Horus was outraged.

The furious young man swore a solemn oath that he would punish his wicked uncle and take his rightful place as king.

From that moment on, Horus thought of nothing else but challenging Seth for the throne. Gossip spread through the whole country about the hot-headed son of Osiris who wanted to fight Seth. The gods and goddesses held an emergency meeting to try to sort out the trouble that was brewing. Everyone was there – except for the mighty Ra, but the gods and goddesses couldn't wait. They went ahead and agreed that Horus was the rightful heir to the throne. Just as they were about to announce their decision, Ra burst in. He was furious at not having been consulted.

'I support Seth,' he roared, just to be awkward.

No one could make the stubborn Ra change his mind, even though the gods and goddesses quarrelled and argued for hours.

'Stop!' Seth and Horus finally shouted. 'We've had enough of all this squabbling. We'll sort it out ourselves!'

Seth and Horus decided to face each other in a series of challenges. They agreed that the overall winner would become the king of Egypt, once and for all.

The first fight was to take place in the River Nile.

The gods and goddesses stood on the banks and watched nervously as Seth and Horus turned into fierce hippopotami.

The snorting animals plunged through the deep waters and attacked each other. They locked huge jaws and bit each other with vicious teeth. The splashing, churning waters ran red with blood. In the end, each hippopotamus fell, exhausted. The gods and goddesses sighed with frustration. There was no clear winner.

After the disappointment of the first contest, Seth decided he'd had enough of fighting fair. He went back to his sneaky ways to try to beat Horus. Seth waited until Horus had fallen asleep, then he crept up quietly and ripped out one of the handsome young man's eyes. Luckily for Horus, the other gods were horrified by this. They told Seth that the victory didn't count and used magic to make Horus' eye well again. The frustrated Seth stormed back to his palace, fuming with anger.

It was in fact Horus who tried to cheat in the next contest. He cunningly suggested to Seth that they should have a boat race – but this would be no ordinary race. The boats had to be made of stone.

Seth was surprised at this suggestion, as he had no idea how to build a stone boat that would be able to float.

But Horus certainly seemed to know the secret and Seth wasn't about to be outdone.

'Great idea!' Seth agreed, smiling nervously.

On the day of the competition, Seth heaved his stone boat down to the Nile to find that Horus had already launched his and was afloat. Horus gave Seth a cheery wave as he bobbed up and down on the water. Horus' boat looked no heavier than a log. Seth gulped and pushed his own boat out into the Nile. It sank straight to the bottom of the river in a matter of seconds.

'I win! I win!' cried Horus gleefully, as the red-faced Seth clambered, dripping, out of the river.

'Not so fast!' bellowed the great god Ra. 'I declare the contest unjust once again!'

The lord of the gods knew everything – and he knew that Horus' boat wasn't really stone at all. It was wood covered with rough plaster, painted to look like stone. As Horus' face fell, Seth wiped the waterweed from his hair and grinned with relief. They were still even...

And so the contests went on. For eighty long years, Seth and Horus were at war with each other, battling out their argument. And still there was no winner! The Egyptian people were tired of the fighting and their beautiful country had been ripped apart by all the battles.

The gods and goddesses longed for peace and quiet.

Finally, Ra's mother had had enough. 'I rule that Horus must become king,' she announced. 'If anyone argues, I will bring the heavens crashing down and end the world.'

The Egyptian people heaved a huge sigh of relief. At last the country had a king once again! The gods and goddesses smiled with joy to see Horus and Seth at peace at last. Even Seth himself was secretly quite happy – he'd had more than enough of all the fighting and was really quite glad to have an excuse to stop.

Horus ruled a contented land for many years, the first in a long line of great rulers called the pharaohs.

Pharaoh and the Thief

There was once a pharaoh who was so rich he didn't know what to do with all his treasure. His palace overflowed with gold and silver furniture and statues. There were boxes of rare spices, bottles of exotic perfumes and enormous chests of precious gems and jewellery. Pharaoh's greatest fear was thieves, so he ordered a special treasure house to be built to keep everything in. It had to be big enough to hold all his riches and impossible to break into.

Eventually, the top-secret building was finished. The architect who had planned and built it held his breath nervously while Pharaoh inspected it. It was just one large room with no windows and only one door. The ceiling, floor and walls were made of solid stone. Pharaoh smiled. It was just right.

Pharaoh's servants packed the building with treasure and heaved the door tightly shut. Pharaoh stamped his royal seal on the entrance. Now no one could get in without breaking the seal, so Pharaoh would know about it. Last of all, Pharaoh set guards outside the door. He then went contentedly back to his palace.

Years passed and now and then Pharaoh went to the treasure house to admire his wonderful fortune. Each time, he was delighted to find everything just as he had left it... That is, until he visited a few days after the architect had died. This time, as Pharaoh looked around, his face fell. He had the funniest feeling that things were missing, but he couldn't be sure. He had so much treasure, he simply couldn't remember where everything was meant to be!

Pharaoh left with a face like a thunder cloud. He set a new seal on the door and stormed back to the palace. After worrying about his treasure for a whole week, Pharaoh returned to the building. The seal was still in place, but when Pharaoh opened the door, he found huge gaps where statues and ornaments were missing. This time he was certain – he had been robbed!

Pharaoh roared with anger and frustration.

'The thief has surprised me, so now I'm going to surprise him!' he fumed.

Pharaoh hid several traps among his treasure and once again sealed the door. Then he spent a sleepless night wondering if the thief had broken in.

Next morning, the seal was still in place, but when Pharaoh went inside, he was baffled. A thief had indeed been caught in one of his traps – but the man had no head!

However did the thief get in? Pharaoh puzzled. *Where is his head? And more importantly, where is my treasure?*

In a rage, Pharaoh hung the thief's body high on the palace walls as a warning to all other robbers.

'Set guards around the body so no one can come and rescue it for burial!' he commanded.

Early next morning, the guards shuffled into the palace, red-faced and trembling.

'O Pharaoh, be merciful!' they cried, falling to their knees. 'Last night, a merchant offered us some free wine. We all got drunk and fell fast asleep. When we woke up, the thief's body was gone!'

'W-H-A-A-T?' Pharaoh roared. 'You fell for that old trick?' He was beside himself with rage. 'I shall outwit this clever thief, no matter what!' he vowed.

Pharaoh came up with a brilliant plan. He announced that the person who could tell his daughter the cleverest secret – no matter how wicked it was – would win her hand in marriage. Pharaoh was sure that the thief would boast to the princess about his daring crime. When he did, the princess would grab his hand and yell for the guards.

Sure enough, the thief soon crept to see the princess. His face was shadowed by a huge hood and his body was hidden by a great cloak.

'My father was the architect of Pharaoh's treasure house,' the thief whispered, 'and just before he died, he told my brother and me a secret. One of the stones in the wall of the treasure house is split in half. It's so neat that you can't see the join. From the outside, you can slide the halves apart and crawl in through the gap.'

The princess' eyes opened wide in amazement.

'My brother and I broke in several times and stole things,' the thief continued, 'but then your father noticed and laid the traps. My poor brother got caught and there was no way to escape. He couldn't bear to face the punishment of a slow, painful death. So he made me finish him off quickly by cutting off his head. I ran away with it, so no one would recognize him and trace us. Then I tricked the guards and rescued his body too.'

The thief's sad face suddenly brightened.

'Isn't that the cleverest secret you've ever heard?' he asked.

'Oh, by far!' the princess agreed – and she meant it. 'You may kiss my hand,' she said.

As soon as the thief took the princess' hand, she gripped tightly and yelled, 'Guards! Come quickly!' But her cries rapidly turned into screams of terror.

The thief had run away into the night – leaving the princess holding a cold, lifeless hand that he must have stolen from a corpse waiting to be buried!

Once again, the thief had beaten Pharaoh. He had known he was walking into a trap, but he had worked out a way to escape. Pharaoh couldn't help being full of admiration for the cunning robber. He sent messengers through Egypt offering the thief a full pardon. When the clever thief gave himself up, Pharaoh rewarded him, too. Pharaoh gave the thief not only his daughter's hand in marriage, but also a job running the country. After all, he was one of the cleverest people in Egypt!

SHIPWRECKED!

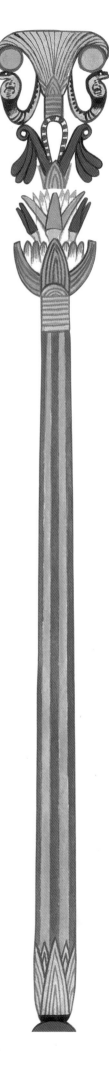

One peaceful night, an Egyptian boat was sailing under
a starry sky. The crew had voyaged to many faraway
lands, searching for treasure. Now the boat had at last
turned for home. As it cut through the waves, the sailors
talked of nothing but their beautiful country of Egypt.
They longed to be back there.

'We should pray to the gods for a safe journey,' one
sailor reminded the rest of the crew. 'Once, I foolishly
forgot that the gods hold all our lives in their hands
and they taught me a lesson I shall always remember!'
The crew listened, wide-eyed, as the sailor told his story.

'I always wanted to be a sailor and was thrilled the
first time I was accepted into a crew. My ship was huge
and elegant. My fellow sailors were well-travelled and
fearless. They knew everything there was to know about
sailing and we all felt sure that our voyage would be safe
and successful.

'But the gods were angry with our pride. They waited
until we were out on the open sea and then stirred up
a terrible storm. The skies turned black and fearsome and
the wind howled around us. Rain lashed us on all sides.

43

Huge waves flung us into the air and dashed us down towards the rocky depths. Our ship was battered and beaten. Finally, a towering wave crashed over us and everyone was swept overboard into the angry waters.

'I was the only person who didn't drown. Perhaps the gods took pity on me because I was so young. The waves washed me up on the shore of a strange island. I was soaked and shivering. I staggered up the beach and collapsed, exhausted, under a pile of soggy driftwood.

'After sleeping for three days and nights, I woke up hungry and thirsty. Luckily, I felt recovered enough to go looking for food and fresh water. To my great delight, I discovered that the island was a lush, green paradise. It was filled with sweet-smelling grasses, flowering bushes and trees laden with juicy fruit. Birds sang in the skies. Animals leapt through the undergrowth. There were sparkling waterfalls and crystal clear pools, filled with fish.

'I thanked the gods for saving my life and bringing me to such a wonderful place. Then I gathered a delicious feast and tucked in.

'While I munched away happily, the ground suddenly began to shake and shudder. Great cracks appeared in the earth and smoke spurted out. Then I heard a dreadful slithering, hissing noise growing louder behind me.

I spun round and screamed out in fear. A giant snake was sliding out of the forest and heading straight for me! The enormous creature was terrifyingly beautiful. It had scales as gold as the sun and as blue as the sea. Most strange of all, the snake had a long beard just like a god's.

'I stood rooted to the spot as the snake reared up, ready to strike. I shut my eyes and waited for its deadly bite. But to my utter amazement, the snake didn't hurt me. It picked me up in its jaws and carefully carried me back to its home, where it set me gently on the ground.

'What happened next was even more surprising. The snake actually spoke to me!

'"You were right to give thanks to the gods," the snake told me, in a soft, rich voice. "They have brought you here to live with me for four months. I will look after you well and after that time, you will be rescued by a passing ship and taken safely back to Egypt. You will live to a ripe old age and die happily in your homeland."

'I was still a little afraid of the magnificent creature, but I was amazed by his gentleness. I fell to my knees and managed to stutter a reply.

'"My lord, when I return to Egypt I will be sure to tell the pharaoh of your kindness. I will ask him to send you many splendid gifts."

'A deep rumble came from the snake's throat and I realized he was laughing. He wisely knew that I was only a common sailor and that I would never be allowed to meet the pharaoh.

'"Thank you, but I don't need your gifts," the snake chuckled. "I am the Prince of Punt and this is my island – the island of Ka. I have a hundred times more riches here than in the whole of the pharaoh's treasure house. The best thing you can give me is your company."

'After that, the snake prince and I became firm friends. We walked and talked every day and enjoyed the beauty of the island, which I soon learned was enchanted. The prince and I told each other stories and played games. We swapped jokes and riddles. When a ship landed on the island after four months and rescued me, I felt extremely sad as well as happy.

'"I promise I will come back one day to see you," I called to the prince as the ship sailed away.

'The mighty snake stood on the shore, watching me leave and his gentle voice floated back to me on the wind.

'"You will never find this place again," he called. "Goodbye, my friend!"'

The sailor sighed.